Written by Eugene F.

Illustrated by Meredith Wolting

To the next graduating class of explorers, you're gonna be great.

"**When they announced that I'll be visiting the 'little blue planet',
I thought that name came from its oceans.
It turned out, this planet is mostly holding its breath.**"

- Alvar0, Team Lead, Star Delivery

The Galactic Federation (GF) saying about Earth was that it was the place where dreams were made real. The planet itself was typical, but the infinite hoard of collectibles that had been placed upon it was mind boggling. There was music to listen to, movies to watch, books to read, and transcendent works of art to ponder over. This was all thanks to humanity. Humans were deemed brilliantly creative, but they were also known to be incredibly dangerous to deal with. It was like a nest of baby bunnies, except the bunny was also a multi-headed dragon. Since the universe enjoyed what Earthlings were making, there was a general rule to simply leave it be.

Earth's first visitors had sent back some strange observations. It was found that after humanity discovered the explosion, there were explosions occurring on a routine basis. Only a few brave researchers remained while the majority of the universe preferred to stay a respectable distance of at least nine or ten light years away. Occasionally, researchers would request assistance, and that was how Star Delivery was born.

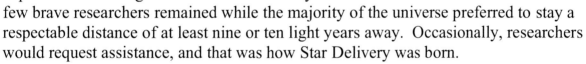

Earth would be added to a list of intergalactic delivery destinations. It would also be the hardest, as it required staying undetected by the native inhabitants. As expected, the job was given to the Botozians. Botozians are a sentient race of robots originating from the planet Botoz. The average Botozian robot stood about three inches tall, weighed less than two pounds and could be trained for the task in the time it takes to boil water in a vacuum space-kettle. They might have been small but they were very good at what they did.

Many robots signed up for Star Delivery and were tested for intelligence, reflexes and coordination. The three robots who received the highest scores would be given personality upgrades to mimic the planet's inhabitants. Arms and legs were added, although this did not make them very much taller. The idea was to give the crew a means to blend in, however in this case, it caused the robots to party wildly during their night of graduation. They wandered about town fascinated with their new arms and legs, having to communicate through speech and this strange desire to eat cookies late at night.

Once on mission, it took a few weeks of traveling across the universe before the robots made it to Earth. The saucer ship stopped above the planet and tooted out a large black cloud. This was one of many displays the galactic federation used to signal other ships. Different coloured clouds represented different movements: black clouds for stop, bright yellow to say hello, and bursts of fire was the universal signal to show that the ship was in trouble. Nine times out of ten, it was on fire.

Inside, a huge green check mark flashed onto the main screen. The robots inside cheered. The crew tossed the things they were holding in triumph. This caused a lot of crashes and broken glass but they were too happy to notice.

"This is the right planet!" said Alvar0, "And it only took us **eight** tries to find it! Nova, Alex, you're both amazing!"

Replacements for their broken equipment had already materialized thanks to the onboard replicators. In fact, the replicators could create anything the crew wanted. They could create complex equipment, replacement parts and more! The only limit the replicators had was that everything they made tasted like chicken. One quickly printed out a list of broken items. Alvar0, the mission lead and pilot, had broken his keyboard in half in celebration. Nova, who handled sensors, generated a new monitor. Alex, the data analyst, had purposely thrown a chair just to get a new one.

"I thought we were going to give up looking." said Alex.

"I only give up when 'Giving Up' is written on our to do list." said Alvar0. "That and we've got a great chance here. We can make a piece of art and give that to humanity! It'll be thanks for all the fun we've had watching them!"

Alex and Nova nodded at the idea before noticing that Alvar0 was standing frozen. He stood in awe of the image of Earth. His eyes had glossed over. Although he had prepared himself for this moment, being there still overwhelmed him.

"Alvar0?" asked Nova. She bounced an empty can on his head when he shook awake.

"Look at that gigantic planet. It's just like in the movies." said Alvar0. "I bet humans are screaming at music concerts. Nova, begin the scan for the client. He's probably marching in a parade or something."

The Earth monitor's readings didn't make any sense. Nova slapped the side of it, so hard that it tilted momentarily on its side before thumping back down. 'Target Not Found' flashed again. She hit the monitor a second time and then began waving a hand in panic.

"Alvar-Zero, the client's location isn't popping up! I suggest we do a close range planetary sweep." said Nova as she picked the monitor up off her desk and shook it.

Alvar0 checked the mission log for the client's name. It read "Elon Mollusc" and under occupation in bold was written, "Shapeshifting Researcher".

"We need to follow protocol. We're not supposed to go down except for the target drop off point." said Alvar0. "Could Elon be hiding?"

"He shouldn't be hiding from us." said Nova. "We've got his stuff."

"Try a pattern search." said Alvar0. "Maybe he left something coded."

Nova untied several cords from her hair. The co-pilot had installed long data cables onto her head which she bundled together to look like hair. She unravelled two cables and plugged herself into the monitor on her lap. Images cascaded quickly across the screen.

"Alex, what can you tell us about the current tech status?" asked Alvar0 as he looked over the planet data. "This planet is a mess. Humans seemed to have done a lot more damage than we expected."

Alex was quick with the scan readouts. "The reports were accurate. Humanity is a Class Zero civilization with Red level tech. I'm also seeing a lot of other data being passed around now that we're here. Oh, I'm also downloading a lot of new movies."

"Nice." smiled Alvar0.

"From the looks of it, the latest signals that reached Botoz were from 15 years ago. The amount of new content available now is crazy. So many new video games too."

4

"Alvar0." interrupted Nova, her voice raised in alarm, her head turned every so often as search images zipped by. "Humanity is missing!"

"The humans are what?" Alvar0 twisted his head about. "How can they be missing?"

"The humans aren't showing up on the scanners!" said Nova, a bit of panic echoing in her voice.

Alvar0 checked his own scanners to confirm. The movie theatres were quiet, restaurants were empty and no festivals were painting the streets red. The humans weren't loitering around coffee shops. There was even less smog in the air.

"Can you check the news feeds?" Nova asked Alex. With a quick murmur of agreement from Alex, the main viewscreen updated to an ominous word that had been attached to thousands of news articles.

"COVID 19"

"What in the world is that?" asked Nova.

"COVID 19 is also known as SARS-COV-2 that was discovered in 2019." said Alex. "It was a zoonotic disease that evolved from a wild coronavirus."

The screen updated to show what a coronavirus looked like. It was a spherical cell covered with club-shaped spikes like those found on the top of a crown.

"I don't understand any of this." said Alvar0.

"It's a disease. A fast one." said Alex.

"Where is the virus located?" asked Nova. "Maybe Elon is hiding from that area."

"It's..." Alex inhaled, "everywhere. It's a global pandemic."

"Everywhere?" said Nova as she went through the ship's memory on infectious diseases, "This thing sounds like a Class 5 virus."

Alex continued, "Symptoms range greatly. Some humans have trouble breathing, with coughing and fever while other humans might not display symptoms at all. The method of transfer is from the aerosols that humans produce."

"Aerosols." repeated Alvar0.

"They're tiny little droplets that can hang in the air. Like, viral paragliders."

"Droplets! That's all that humans make! Humans are sprinkler systems of wet gas!"

Alvar0 paced back and forth. Nova pulled the cables on her head taunt from stress.

Nova stood up. "This IS a Class Five virus! They don't have the technology to cure this! This thing has destroyed other planets!"

Alex and Alvar0 stared blankly.

"The humans are missing because they're all dead!" shouted Nova. She grabbed her monitor and threw it across the room.

"I hate to say it, but I think you might be right. Humanity finally punched their last ticket." said Alvar0. "Arguably it was just a matter of time that they did something really stupid, but a viral pandemic could also take them out."

An emotion bubbled up inside Nova and she felt a tear run down her cheek. She looked up to see Alvar0 and Alex had begun to tear up as well. A moment later, tears were arcing across the room in all directions as the robots wept.

"I'll miss the humans." said Alvar0.

"They made the best movies!" said Alex.

"I really liked their music scene!" Nova cried, until another loud ding came from the main viewscreen. It was the outline of a human body with a green check mark beside it.

"Humans!" the robots shouted in unison.

"They're still alive!" said Nova, who wiped her tears with a materialized handkerchief.

"They're easy to kill but hard to die!" said Alvar0. "Why didn't the system recognize them?"

"Our facial recognition program didn't connect. Maybe their faces melted off?" said Alex.

"Yech. Could that be a virus thing?" said Nova. "But they're alive and that's what matters!"

"I'm not sure how. They don't have the technology to make a Class 5 Vaccine." Alvar0 interjected, "Could the sensors be making a mistake?"

"Can we check up close?" asked Nova.

"It's on the to do list!" said Alvar0 as he excitedly switched the engines back on. Clouds of white smoke gathered at the back of the spaceship. He pushed the controls causing the saucer to descend. A loud clang echoed off from beneath the ship.

"What was that?" asked Alex.

"You've just knocked a satellite out of orbit!" said Nova.

"I... meant to do that," said Alvar0 as the ship flew into another. "Maybe this will get Elon's attention."

More clamouring bangs could be heard as the saucer struck additional satellites out of orbit.

"How was this supposed to signal the client?" asked Nova.

"I'm not sure?" said Alvar0. "But I am getting pretty good at it - I've easily knocked a dozen satellites out of orbit already."

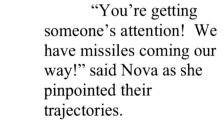

"You're getting someone's attention! We have missiles coming our way!" said Nova as she pinpointed their trajectories.

The blips on the screen were approaching quickly. Alvar0 tapped several keys and the ship veered.

"Alex, jam the missiles to hit each other!" said Alvar0. "Is this some kind of automated defence?"

"I don't think so." said Nova. "The humans are definitely alive and they are definitely still very dangerous!"

"I'm jamming." said Alex.

"Humans. Destroy a few billion dollar satellites and they try to shoot you down." said Alvar0. The ship darted about in sharp angles as a small explosion trailed behind it. The vessel weaved a final loop before it descended through the atmosphere.

"I think they've lost track of us. There's nothing else coming." said Nova.

"Look out humans, here we come!" shouted Alvar0 triumphantly.

The saucer took rest over one of the computer's listed population centers. It was a mid-sized city with only a couple high-rises near its center. The saucer's detection system had focused on a lone human man who was going out for a jog. He mostly stared at the ground and was listening to a set of wireless headphones.

"Oh wow, humans are big!" shouted Nova as she zoomed the camera about the man. "They're sweaty flesh giants."

"I'm correcting our search parameters. We had a lot of it wrong." said Alex as they checked the analysis. "Humans aren't made of sugar and spice after all. It's mostly just sugar."

"Why is he running? There aren't any predators out." said Nova.

"I don't know but I can ascertain this much, humans are nothing like our original estimates." said Alvar0.

Humans as biological entities, were not given much scrutiny. There are millions of planets with life. If you chose one randomly and took closer inspection, you would find that most of that life was squishy and very self-centered. There would be very few creatures interested in dedicating their life to studying other species. And only a subset of those would be interested in actually moving to another world. Of that fraction of off world researchers, only the most brave would be willing to go to a place like Earth. To summarize, the robots had been given bad data and only now that they were a few feet away from an actual human did they realize it.

Another reason why humans were so forgettable was due to the fact they were such great innovators of entertainment. Nova described it as listening to birds sing but not caring which bird was which. The music was all that mattered.

With their sensors recalibrated, the alien robots were now able to track humanity both indoors and out. The initial results were puzzling.

"Why are the humans grouped together inside and then far apart when outside?" asked Alvar0. "We weren't trained about this. Is it something that happens when you get infected with the virus?"

The robot pointed to several samples where humans were standing in lines outdoors. They were spaced evenly and standing on markers on the ground.

"That voluntary separation does happen with older humans. It's called farting." said Alex.

"They're not farting. They're doing it to avoid getting infected." said Nova. "Or maybe it is to avoid getting farted on. Alex, can you find anything about this?"

Alex put a fist to their chin and scanned the internet. The robot usually took various positions of thinking whenever they did a scan.

"They've created a habit called social distancing. They're staying six feet apart from each other." said Alex. "They try to follow this rule whenever they go outside their social bubble."

"What's a social bubble?"

"It's the people they can't avoid or choose not to avoid. Friends and family mostly."

Humans needed to get out often to survive. To buy food or supplies and in rare instances, to exercise. There were many more people who left homes to keep processes working. Individuals who kept the essential services running and thus maintained the survival of those around them.

Of course, very similar to many aliens, some humans acted out of self-interest. There were hoarders. In one image, it was a man pushing a shopping cart that had been loaded with goods.

"Look at that one! He's trying to buy all the toilet paper!" remarked Nova.

"That's going to be a problem for that one that is buying all the coffee and bran muffins." said Alvar0.

As the robots amused themselves over the human's antics, Nova and Alvar0 bumped shoulders against each other. A bit surprised, they began to slowly back away from each other.

"You two need to separate more to be considered socially distanced." said Alex. "Height isn't a factor. It needs to be 6 feet apart. That's two metres."

There was a small pause as they looked at the floor and at the distance between the two.

"Look at us! We're humans!" they said. They raised their little arms in triumph. Their minds began to rewrite lessons they had prepared for the mission.

"So, if I'm infected here, you'll be fine over there!" said Nova.

The two robots waved their arms in front of themselves as if they were slap fighting each other from six feet away.

"Wait a Zeptosecond! When humans talk, they are spraying aerosols into the air." Alvar0 added. "We need to test this."

A soft hum of the replicators generated several bottles of blue dye for the robots to play with. Alvar0 poured a cup's worth of liquid into his mouth and set his internal mechanisms to exhale as he spoke again.

"I'm a normal human, and I am spitting at you." said Alvar0 as brightly colored mist sprayed from his mouth. It splashed harmless on the floor and tables, barely missing the other robots.

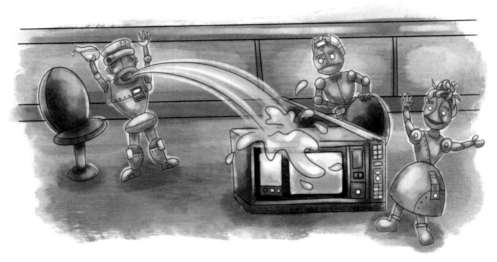

Nova upturned the entire bottle and poured its contents into her mouth. "I'm speaking moistly!" laughed Nova as she spoke, and a spray of liquid shot out of her mouth and nose. Dye dripped off her entire body and onto her workstation and the floor. "Oops, I think I just sneezed."

"This is getting gross." said Alex, who took shelter behind a chair and opened a quickly materialized umbrella.

As Alvar0 reached for another bottle, Nova took a step closer to grab one for herself.

"A… achoo!" shouted Nova as liquid splashed in all directions. The dye did a satisfying arc through the air where it immediately splashed onto Alvar0's face.

"Whoops." said Nova as she looked down. In her excitement she had closed the distance between them by a couple feet. Alvar0 wiped his eyes while Alex took notes.

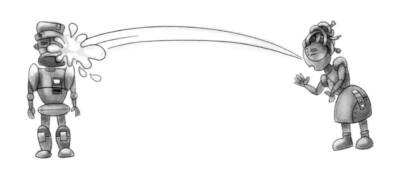

"This doesn't work. It's easy to misjudge how far apart you are." said Alex as they lowered their umbrella. "That, and humans can't stand in place all day - they'll eventually be too close."

"I must agree, for I have been successfully infected." said Alavar0 as he grabbed a towel and wiped the dye off his face.

"Then what's the secret?" asked Nova as she bounced back to her seat. Small splashes of dye flew around her as she fumbled with her hair to reconnect to the system. "Social distancing isn't the complete answer."

"I feel so funky..." said Alvar0 as he sat back down at his station and tossed the wet towel on the floor. "I'm surprised humans were willing to stand near each other before the virus."

Humanity had a history of being rather territorial. The original assumptions behind this was that humans enjoyed being naked too often. There were warning stories about encountering 'naked grandma' and the horror that it caused the neighbours. Thus, the invention of the wall became commonplace. It protected humans from the outside and they could also draw on it.

This theory extended to a subconscious fear of new viral invaders. It was tribal in nature. Individuals present would be considered safe, but possible contaminations from others was a very primal instinct. According to the calculations, it was a surprise that anyone got along.

"I've found their secret! Look!" said Alex as the viewscreen image changed to a young woman on the main screen.

Alex zoomed in on the woman's face. She was wearing a black cotton mask that covered her nose and mouth. It was held in place by elastics looped behind her ears and the mask cupping below her jawline.

Alvar0 scratched his head at the image. It still didn't seem to be accurate, however this did explain why none of the facial recognition software was working.

"A mask like that could block some moisture going in." Alvar0 guessed. "But it doesn't seem to block out viruses."

"They could fix it pretty easily. They just need to use some self-sealing adhesives so no air can pass back and forth." said Alex.

"That can't be right. The masks aren't meant to kill the user." said Alvar0. "And how would they eat?"

"I get it!" said Nova, "The masks are being used like a net. They're not trying to protect themselves but to control what they're breathing out. They're catching the aerosols while they're spitting them out."

"Masks make a huge difference statistically. They have made millions of masks and they've made a lot of designs." said Alex. "I'll make some samples!"

Replicators began generating dozens of masks and soon the floor was covered in them. There were masks in different shapes, sizes and colours. As the pile of masks reached almost as tall as Alex, Alvar0 forced the replicators to stop.

"That's a big pile of masks." marvelled Alvar0.

The robot grabbed a mask similar to the one seen on the viewscreen. He held it up and examined its design.

"This one is black!" he said as he held up a cotton mask.

"This one is cute and blue!" said Nova as she wore a surgical mask on her head.

"I've got a red one that fits under my chin!" said Alex as they put one around their neck.

The robots took turns trying the masks on. It would appear that putting them on incorrectly was a very natural mistake. At first the robots tried covering the eyes, ears and mouth. They wore the masks under the nose, under the jaw and a dozen other different ways, but none felt correct. On the other hand, the robots didn't breathe either. It was Nova who compared herself to the woman they saw earlier.

"We're wearing them fashionably but what we're doing is wrong." Nova said, "The mask, according to the scans made, goes over the nose and mouth."

"So the parts humans expect air to come out of." said a masked Alvar0.

"Just on the face." said Nova as she pulled a mask off her backside.

"I still haven't found a mask I like." said Alex who was now crawling through the various mountains of cloth. Alex emerged with another mask on their face, this one with stars.

"Do I look like a human now?" asked Alex from behind the pile of masks.

Nova climbed up the pile to peer over.

"You look exactly like a human!" said Nova. "Except possibly, more competent."

"Let me see!" Alvar0 said as he stood up on Nova's table for a better view. His foot slipped on blue dye and he landed face down onto the table. Wet once again, Alvar0 had blue dye dripping from his arms.

"I got the virus from the table?" he said annoyed. The robot lifted an arm and let the liquid slide down his elbow. "Is this a thing?"

"I'm afraid it is. The virus can last for several hours on some surfaces." said Alex. "And humans touch a lot of the same items. Doorknobs, handrails, tables. Touch is a very important sense."

"Yes, but how do they avoid this?" asked Alvar0 as he showed his blue palm.

"Actually, they don't."

"They don't?"

"No, they assume they have picked up the virus and wash their hands for 20 seconds. Or if they can't do that, they'll use hand sanitizer."

"Wash hands?!" said Alex, confused.

"It's a vile habit. They cover their hands with soap and water. It's meant to scrub off any dirt or germs that are on their hands." said Nova.

"We need one of those things they wash their hands in." Alvar0 replied.

"It's called a sink! I've found plenty on sale on the internet." said Alex. "In fact, I've found one forest website that sells almost everything."

"Should we buy one?"

"2-3 weeks delivery."

"Aw forget it, let's just use the replicator." Alvar0 said as Nova checked the ship's controls.

Nova was now sitting back in her chair, a mask properly fitted to her face. The viewscreen was flashing several warnings. She stopped as her eyes scanned the local radar with several blips in the air.

"Alvar0, we've been found again!" said Nova. "It looks like several jets are coming this way to investigate us."

"I guess we better jet too!!" said Alvar0. He flipped the engines on and the saucer shot off across the sky. After putting some distance between the ship and the advancing scouts, the robots had taken refuge at the base of the Rocky Mountains.

"Any signs of pursuit?" asked Alvar0.

"I think we lost them." said Nova as she flipped through some readouts. "I think we accidentally triggered their radar. Some countries have locked down international travel to control the virus too!"

"I'm going to do a quick scout of the area." said Alvar0 as he flew between two mountain peaks. He slowed as he passed a large cliffside underneath a hill of snow. He stopped the saucer and reversed. There wasn't anyone nearby and this might be his only chance.

"I've always wanted to leave some art behind for the Earthlings." said Alvar0, eyeing the blank canvas before him. "Imagine it, Botozians leaving art for the Earth to enjoy."

Nova smirked.

"We wouldn't be the first. In fact, it's a known phenomenon here. Other visitors have created the Nazca lines, crop circles, and community theatre. We can leave something behind too!" said Alex.

"I'm going to replicate a drawing utensil on the hull of the ship." said Alvar0 as he typed onto his keyboard. A large double-barrelled laser materialized. With a fast trigger, Alvar0 fired lasers onto the side of the mountain.

"Hah! Everyone should recognize this." Alvar0 said as he finished. It was a line drawing of the face of a large distorted cat. Its tongue was sticking out on one side in defiance. A word bubble emanated from the cat, reading, "Meow humans!"

As Alvar0 tilted the ship back to reposition for his signature, he twisted the laser altering "Meow humans!" into a "Me < 3 Humans".

"That's actually better." said Alvar0 as he completed his work.

"I'm getting a signal!" said Nova.

"The humans are back? Are there more jets? Drones? Super Soldiers with jetpacks?"

"No. It's the client!" said Nova.

The co-ordinates pointed to a location deep below the Pacific Ocean. After roaring over the waves and avoiding other planes in search of them, the saucer plunged into the blue. This surprised an aggregation of manatees which then quickly forgot the incident happened.

"All this water makes me want to wash our hands." said Nova. As she spoke, a spout materialized on a nearby wall. The replicator had created an outside faucet normally found attached to houses. Before any of the robots could correct the error, water began to flow directly onto the bridge. Nova stuck her hands out underneath the stream and began energetically washing her hands. Alvar0 raised a digit in silent protest but was struck in awe of the strange ritual that humans performed. Alex helped clarify the instructions of what to do.

"Wash with soap for twenty seconds." repeated Nova. "Get a really good lather! Scrub your fingertips, thumbs and the back of the hands too."

As the water stopped, a blue checkmark appeared on the viewscreen. The robots cheered in joy. It was the client, signalling that it saw the saucer.

The saucer dove deeper into the dark middle depths of the ocean.

On the dark seabed below, the client Elon was waving a bright light in one of his arms. Elon quivered about as the delivery started to get near and he began to emotionally gyrate. He was a bright green cephalopod whose eyes reflected light from the saucer. His own body gave off a light glow as they approached.

"Dropping the cargo!" said Alex as a big drone filled with off-world foods labelled 'Star Delivery' launched from beneath the ship. Alvar0 guided the food drone to the squid's waiting arms. As it landed, Elon happily pressed a button on a small device for confirmation.

"Another meal delivered!" said Nova as she gave a quick clap of her hands.

"Alex, do the humans know that Elon here is studying them?" Alvar0 asked.

"No, but what they do know is fascinating. Apparently, humans know that cephalopods are so different from everything else that they call them the aliens from Earth."

"If only they knew the truth." joked Nova.

"They definitely have a lot of interesting opinions on the topic." said Alex.

Opinions from humans, similar to aerosols, and were often spread without invitation and to calamitous results.

"Let's go home." said Alvar0 as he ascended through the oceans toward the surface. The saucer floated and slowed. There was a large group of humans wandering the beach and picking up trash that had been washed ashore. Alvar0 stopped the ship so they could examine the bizarre behaviour.

"They're cleaning," said Nova, a bit puzzled. "They don't live in the water. They're cleaning it for the fish?"

Alvar0 looked about the ship and saw spills, masks and hoards of broken equipment on the ground. Despite the huge task, he felt the urge to follow what he saw.

"We should clean the ship."

"But it isn't our job." said Alex. "We have robots programmed to do that when we get back."

"I want to try it." said Nova as she picked up a pile of masks.

Soon all three robots were picking things up off of the ground. They piled things up in rows and again by material until they realized that holding onto everything was simply another part of the trash. A large recycling bin that could absorb materials back into energy was quickly created.

As the final pieces were recycled, Nova examined the fuel gage. "Now we have more than enough fuel to get back home."

The robots stood as they pondered this solution they had missed. Perhaps this simple world had something to learn from.

"Nova, do you have a complete map of everywhere we travelled?" asked Alvar0. "Including all the satellites we knocked out of orbit?"

"Yes. We've knocked 27 satellites out of orbit." said Nova. Alvar0 took a deep breath.

"I'm going to put them back." said Alvar0. He reprogrammed the saucer and it took flight faster than it had ever gone before. As the ship placed satellites back into their original orbits, Alvar0 considered whether they should break a major rule that they were given.

"Alex. Can we design a vaccine for the disease?" asked Alvar0.

"Of course we can." said Alex.

"Let's quietly upload it into their systems."

Alex paused for a moment as they searched global databases once again. The robot's eyes danced about in thought. Then they stared ahead as if looking through the hull and onto the vastness of space.

"Any luck?" asked Alvar0.

"They already have it. There have been dozens of countries in laboratories across the world researching vaccines. They just need to finish the stages of testing."

Alvar0 placed an image of a nearby city on the viewscreen. It had dozens of high-rise buildings, bright lights and a tower near its harbourfront. The city spoke as if in testament that humanity was growing in a manner that they did not conceive of. Alvar0 turned the monitor off as he addressed the rest of the crew.

"Do you know the real reason why Botozians get more shipping missions than any other planet?" asked Alavr0.

"I'd like to say it's because we're the best, but I think you're going to tell us something else." said Nova.

"It's because others are afraid of cross planetary viral infections. It takes years, sometimes decades of research to confirm whether it is safe for two planets to interact with each other. I think this Earth's low tech approach might be something we can bring back." said Alvar0.

Thus, was born the invention of Protocol One. A means for alien species to greet each other with minimal odds of passing viruses from far off planets. They would meet in specific locations. They practiced social distancing, wore masks and kept attention to cleanliness. They would also clean up the equipment and gear that they used.

When the time finally came, vaccines would be introduced and the galaxy would finally be able to take a breath. Together.

"Earth. Social Distance with it. If you land here, wear a mask. Wash frequently. Don't leave any mess behind. But most of all, keep an eye on them because they're going to do great things."

-   Alex, Head Researcher and Data Analyst, Star Delivery

Made in the USA
Monee, IL
16 April 2021